Statty Sticks

Peter Marney

ISBN-13: 978-1975674823

ISBN-10: 1975674820

This book is dedicated to tolerance and understanding, may they ever increase.

Read this first

You are not a ninja.

It's very important that you keep remembering this.

If you try to copy any of the stuff in this book then you might end up in prison.

Even if you copy just some of this stuff, you'll end up in trouble.

This will be bad.

This will be very bad because I'll get the blame.

So please, remember you're not a ninja and promise not to try and copy me.

Have you promised?

Ok, you can now read on.

A new craze

Ouch!

Here I am, sitting on a bench in the playground minding my own business, and I've just been thumped on the head.

Seems to be more dangerous in school now that I'm in Year Five.

What have I done to deserve this?

I'm Jamie by the way and I'm going to have a big bump anytime soon.

1

Did I mention I'm now in Year Five? It's no big deal although Mum says it means I'm a big boy now.

I'm sort of angry but trying not to show it as I don't want to scare the small infant who is shuffling closer but wishing she was somewhere else. I think she's the one who just hit me.

How do these things start?

I mean, a couple of weeks ago I was able to sit here without any chance of being assaulted but now I'm taking my life in my hands.

The reason for this change is a sudden craze for diabolos.

In case you're from another planet or this craze hasn't hit you yet, a diabolo is sort of like one of those sand timers we use in school but in plastic. It's spun by two sticks joined by a piece of string and people can do tricks with them.

I don't think this little one's very good with her tricks yet. I reckon she used her string to throw the diabolo into the air to catch it again but sort of lost control. So instead of coming straight back down, it wandered off and hit me on the head.

I should tell her off but she already looks like she's going to burst into tears so I smile and hand the toy back to her.

"I can't do that trick either," I say, "so maybe it's better if you practise on the field."

She nods and runs off without crying so I think maybe I've done the right thing.

The reason I can't do that trick is because Mum won't buy me a diabolo. Can't say I care much but it would have made a nice late birthday present.

I wonder how these crazes start?

It's like girls and clothes.
They're all wearing jeans and boots
then suddenly something changes and
they've all got to have green tops
or dresses like everyone else.

Is there a secret group somewhere
who decides these things?

Maybe they own a factory which
makes diabolos and green tops but
no, that sounds a bit daft. After
all, diabolos come in all different
colours and I just happen to have
got hit by a green one.

Maybe the knock has jumbled my
thinking. I know when I sort of
fell off of the climbing frame I
had trouble thinking properly for a
day or two even after I came out of
hospital.

I should explain that I was being
a bit stupid as usual and trying to
do a secret ninja trick on my way
through the climbing frame which
we'd been told to stay off of as it
was wet and slippery.

Yes, I'm a ninja but it's supposed to be a secret.

I'm the original Red Sock Ninja although I'm now part of a clan with Wally and Red and I suppose Keira who, being a lot older and much more skilful, is our sort of leader.

That means she's the one who usually gets us into trouble.

We're not bad or anything; it's just that sometimes we need to do some naughty things to make right things happen. It's complicated but it all sort of works out properly in the end and we haven't been caught doing anything wrong yet.

I suppose I should show some interest in this new craze but I can't get excited about throwing something up into the air just to catch it again. You could do that with a tennis ball but I don't see anyone playing catch in the playground this week.

Give it a while and all of these flying weapons will have disappeared and everything will be back to normal.

Maybe the secret committee will invent something new and everyone will do that instead.

Or maybe I could start a new craze and get everybody jumping about on one leg.

No, I'd just look silly and anyway, even if lots of people copied me, someone would only go and fall over and hurt themselves and then I'd get the blame.

Maybe I'll just stick to dodging diabolos for now.

Changes

Miss S, who is still my teacher, has told us that we'll be getting some visitors in school this week and that we're to be polite to them and just carry on as normal.

She says that they want to see what a good school we are and how well we're learning things.

We're used to people popping in and out of our classroom.

Sometimes I get a visit from Mrs Williams who helps me with my reading and we've also got Miss Northgate who helps out in the Year Five and Six classes but Miss says these new visitors are special and important.

I can tell they're important because I start to notice small changes.

Some of the old displays on the boards outside certain classes are suddenly changed and some of the teachers who usually disappear as soon as the bell rings at the end of the day are now staying at their desks and working late.

This isn't acting as normal but I don't think we're supposed to say anything.

My teacher, Miss S isn't making any extra fuss; she always works late and our displays are always changing as we do new work. Some of the other classes only have the very neatest work on their walls but in our class we all get put up there if we've done something good even if it looks a bit grubby.

It's now a few days later and I've worked out that our visitors are a man and two women but we only see one of the women in our class and she only stays for about half of the lesson. I don't know what she can learn in that time although she did ask some of us questions about what we were doing.

If they wanted to know what sort of school this is, you'd have thought that they might ask us what we think of our teachers but they don't. Wally says that our parents have been asked what they think of the school but Mum didn't mention it.

Red is having fun watching her teacher do all sorts of stuff he never usually does. Even the lessons are more interesting this week.

There's also a new kid in Red's class as well who's causing a bit of a fuss because she's got two Mums.

I don't see what's new about this as lots of kids in our school get new Mums or Dads when the old one leaves but Red says that this is different. Naz has got two Mums living together at the same time and there's no Dad.

One or two people on the estate are saying it's wrong but why?

People can live with who they want to and, as long as they're nice and not hurting anyone, why should anyone worry?

After a few days, our visitors leave and everyone goes back to normal. Red's lessons become boring again and half of the teachers cars are gone by the time I leave on Friday night.

I don't see how most people manage to keep all of their things together in school and have everything ready to go home each night. It usually takes me a good ten minutes to find everything and sometimes longer. Some afternoons, if I've really slow, I'm still there when the cleaners come in to tidy up.

Miss also has to keep reminding me to take any letters home as well as I usually forget to take them out of my tray.

She's threatened to staple them to my head if I keep forgetting but I think she's joking.

I wouldn't be able to see properly if I had a letter stapled in front of my eyes and Mum might have to turn me upside down to read it.

As well as noticing the half empty car park I also notice a strange man watching the school. Actually he's pretending not to be watching but he's doing the same sort of things that us Red Socks do when we're secretly spying on someone.

I think about trying to follow him but it's boxing night so I mustn't be late home.

I wonder who he's spying on?

Boxing and babies

I started boxing because Keira got fed up with me always being thrown on the floor during our school judo sessions. She also said I needed to build up my fitness.

I didn't see any problem with my being unfit but it didn't stop Keira dragging me along to the local youth club for boxing lessons.

These lessons are run by Big Jay who is Red's scary cousin. He's not as scary as Red when she gets angry but I try to stay out of the way of both of them if they're being grumpy.

Tonight is ok though and I manage to stay out of the spotlight of Jay's attention by spending some time hitting the big bag. This is the bag which most of us can't move but which Keira got swinging when she aimed a kick at it. She also managed to put Big Jay on his bottom with a kick as well but he did ask for it.

They'd argued about girls training in the gym but as we've now got five of them I guess Keira won that argument. I haven't fought any of them yet but one or two look quite good. I still think that Red would beat all of them though even if she did have to follow the rules.

One of the new girls is Naz and she joins Red and me when we have a break. Red has told me that Naz is nice and I soon find that out for myself.

Like me, Naz has been to a few different schools and moved around a bit. Neither of us like moving much but we agree that this school is a bit better than most. It's a shame that she doesn't have a teacher like Miss S but Red says that perhaps they'll get her next year.

I hadn't thought that I won't always have Miss S as my teacher and the idea of change comes as a bit of a shock.

I'm distracted by it for the rest of the evening which isn't a good thing because, after break, we have practise matches and I keep forgetting to duck and end up getting punched lots.

One of Naz's Mums comes to pick her up and she chats to Keira while we get changed. She seems nice too.

Then we say goodbye and Keira and me start our jog home.

I'd forgotten to tell Keira about the mystery man outside school but it seems a bit silly now so I don't bother. Instead I try and beat her to Mr Patel's shop where we usually stop for a breather and a chat. I think she's letting me win tonight.

Mr Patel is excited as his daughter who lives in India is coming for a visit and bringing her new baby. Mr Patel hasn't seen his new little grandson yet, except on his computer, and he's very happy tonight. He shows us a picture of the little baby and Keira makes the usual girly noises.

Babies all look the same to me, even Wally's baby sister Milly, and they all smell the same too.

Yuk!

Girls seem to like them for some reason and even Red forgets to be normal when she sees one of her baby cousins. I suppose it's all that playing with dolls in the infants that makes them like that.

Mind you, I used to play with dinosaurs a lot but I haven't grown up wanting to cuddle one.

Girls are strange.

I'm thinking all of this while we're jogging home and it's only when we get there that I notice something else as well.

Do you sometimes get the feeling that someone is watching you?

Sometimes in class I'll be working on something when I get this feeling and look up to find Miss S staring at me. She usually smiles and then looks at someone else but I know she's been watching me working.

It's a quiet sort of tugging at my mind and difficult to describe but I'm getting it now. I should maybe tell Keira but it's just a feeling and I can't find anyone to blame it on, so I keep the thought to myself. Maybe I got punched too many times tonight.

I think I'll have to start practising dodging punches in front of our mirror in the bathroom. I used to practise my secret ninja moves there until I fell into the bath and Mum made a fuss so maybe that's not such a good idea.

I fall asleep dodging boxing gloves and making flying kicks at the enemies of the Red Sock Ninja Clan.

Cameras

We've lost George.

I think maybe he's gone for a walk like Harry the goldfish but nobody can find him.

Miss asks all of us whether we've seen George or if anyone took him home for a visit but nobody is owning up. Anyway, I think it'd be a bit difficult to smuggle a big plant like George out of school without someone noticing.

A few days later he's still not reappeared and other things have started to go missing as well. Nothing really important but odd little things like rubbers and paint pots. Some of these reappear in other classrooms but most just stay lost. It doesn't sound like much but it's sort of unsettling.

Something odd is happening and I think the Red Sock Ninjas should investigate.

That's why the four of us are now sneaking around the school in the dark with three spy cameras which Keira has brought with her. We used these cameras for another of our adventures and they're good at spotting things when there's supposed to be nobody about.

Last time we set them up on a rooftop but now we've got to find places where they won't be noticed. It's no good having a secret spy camera if everyone knows where it is.

During the day, the three of us have been searching out possible sites for these cameras and so tonight it's quick and easy to get them in place. One of them can watch the main corridor and entrance while another is watching the playground outside.

I wanted to put the last one in the staff room but Keira won't let me. I've always wanted to know what the teachers do in there all the time. I suppose I'll have to wait until I can find my own camera.

Some of our classes have air vents in the walls and during that day I'd noticed that a few of the grills had fresh screw marks with some of the old paint chipped off.

I notice this sort of thing because I'm a secret ninja and that's just the sort of place I'd want to put a camera, apart from the staff room.

I mention the marks to Keira and she goes very quiet and still.

I hadn't thought about it but maybe someone else has decided to install cameras as well which could be a big problem.

Luckily, we're all in full ninja gear with our hoods up and with the lights off. If these other cameras do exist then they'll need to be able to see in the dark to spot us.

I tell Kiera exactly which classrooms I've seen the marks in and she tells us all to stay away from them. She then unrolls a set of small tools from her pocket and goes into one of the these rooms.

A few minutes later and she reappears, nodding her head.

We've had some unwanted visitors and they've left spies of their own.

We go into full ninja battle mode and start acting as though we have an enemy in the school with us.

We silently spread out with Keira
in the lead and me at the rear. Red
and Wally are ready to attack at
the sides if necessary and we're
watching in all directions.

We decide to exit the school
through one of the infant windows
after checking that the classroom
isn't bugged by any camera. That
puts us near to the trees and
bushes by that part of the school
and will give good cover. From
there we stay in the bushes as much
as we can until we reach a gap in
the fence which we can fit through.

Keira goes first and walks to the
end of the lane, followed by Wally
who goes in the opposite direction.
If either of them whistle then me
and Red are prepared to double back
into the school bushes and find
another way out.

We wait in silence for two
minutes.

Then, slowly, we both exit the
school, remove our hoods and start

to stroll along as if just out for
a walk.

If anyone is watching then running
will only make us look suspicious.
Instead there's just me and Red who
happen to see Keira disappearing
around the corner as we walk along
chatting about the youth club and
boxing.

Wally will be finding his own way
home and we'll all get together in
school tomorrow morning.

Now all I've got to figure out is
how to tell someone about the
cameras without putting the ninjas
or our own cameras in danger.

Unhappy

The playground is buzzing with news.

It seems that our special visitors a while back were school inspectors and they've now written their report.

For some reason, they don't like our school and some parents have read the report on our website and aren't happy either.

Red has seen it and tells me it says that some parents are worried about all the bullying at the school.

This is a surprise because I didn't know we had a problem with bullying and neither does Red or Wally.

Of course there are the odd fights and some name calling but nothing long term and no real bullying that I've seen.

Red's asked a cousin in Year Three and a couple more in the infants and they've not seen anything either.

I wonder who these parents are then?

That day, Mrs Wallace gets some more visitors and Miss S warns us to be polite if they happen to come in our class which they don't. Instead they spend the whole morning in Mrs Wallace's office and she looks a bit red when she comes out at lunchtime.

I get to see this special report a couple of nights later when Keira comes to babysit and brings her computer.

(I know I'm not a baby but I still haven't found a better word for what she does).

She reads it out to me and some of it sounds like they're talking about a different school. I know we're not perfect but not all of our teachers are rubbish and most of us want to learn.

So why is this report so bad?

Keira says that some of the information has been used badly and that some of the stats look a bit iffy as well.

"What's stats?" I ask.

I wish I hadn't.

Keira's explanation gets complicated but basically it's a short word for "Statty Sticks" or something which Keira says means lying with numbers.

I didn't know that numbers could lie and this worries me because one and one should always add up to two. If it starts making three or seven then how am I going to get my sums right in school?

Apparently, these Statty Sticks can mean different things to different people.

"It's like a glass half full of juice Jamie," says Keira.

I give my usual clueless look.

"You can say it's half empty or you can say it's half full. It just depends on your point of view."

I'd not thought about it like that before. To me it's just a glass with some juice in it.

"If you want things to look bad, then you can complain that the glass is always half empty."

I interrupt.

"But it's half full as well, which is a lot better than having nothing at all so it's really a good thing."

I've got the idea now and see that these inspectors are only looking for half empty things.

Our reading is sort of good but not good enough.

Our writing is maybe ok but with some poor pupils. I wonder if that's because they saw my work on our classroom wall? It's a bit grubby but I did my best.

The school's Maths could also be a lot better.

It seems that wherever we've done well, it should be better and where we've done not so well, it's much worse than it should be.

Everyone is getting the blame except the inspectors who I don't think have been very fair.

Keira says that someone has written to the local paper complaining and saying that the school is a disgrace and should be closed down. The letter is signed "An angry parent" which I guess means someone's Mum or Dad.

I think someone ought to write and complain about this unfair report.

I've been to a lot of schools and this is the best one so far and Miss S is the best teacher ever.

That's got to count for something hasn't it?

I mean, how do you judge a school? I'd have thought that having happy pupils would be a good thing and shows that the school is doing something right.

Keira says that the inspectors say that the children don't seem happy and the ones they spoke to weren't really interested in what they were doing.

I think the Red Socks need to start talking to people because that wasn't true in our class. Miss was getting us all to look at our project and we had lots to talk about but none of this seems to have make it into the report.

So where were all these half empty lessons filled with half empty and unhappy kids?

Peter Marney

Strangers

There are more strange people in our school the next week and some of them are looking at our fields as well.

I'm not sure how a field can make a better school unless you start testing climbing frames and goal posts but there must be something to interest these men because they start taking measurements.

I also think I've seen my own mystery man again but I can't be sure.

After school, while I was watching the measuring men, I sort of half caught a glimpse of someone disappearing behind a bush just the other side of the fence. It's more of a feeling but I decide to keep alert in case it happens again.

I tried to follow some of the measuring men when they left but they just climbed into a car and drove off. I wrote the car number on my hand and will know the car if I see it again.

Red's mum has got the Pike family talking to all the school parents but nobody has owned up yet to talking about bullying or writing to the paper.

The Red Socks haven't done any better either.

We've spoken to people in every single class and nobody has told us about unhappy kids or about any boring lessons when the inspectors were here.

A couple of the classes only had them in for ten minutes or so and in one class the woman didn't even talk to anyone. I don't know how you can work out what we're thinking if you don't talk to us.

It's all very odd.

I've been chatting to Naz and she seems happy to be here.

She's turning into a good boxer as well and has been allowed to fight two of the boys, one at a time of course. Jay still wasn't happy about the idea but Keira persuaded him and he watched the fight very carefully to make sure nobody got hurt.

Not that there was much chance of that happening.

Naz is really quick and can dodge about better than me and Red put together. Her punches look strong as well and she managed to put one of the boys onto his bottom with a right hook punch to the side of his helmet. That was when Jay stopped the fight and declared her the winner.

Naz told me that she used to be bullied at school when she was little so one of her Mums took her to boxing lessons.

Her Mum also argued with the Head when Naz got told off for punching the bully on the nose. Naz didn't get bullied any more though so I guess it worked.

I don't think I'd want to try and bully anyone who punched me on the nose. Not that I'd want to bully anyone anyway.

Actually I don't know why anyone would want to be a bully. Maybe it's so they can look tough and scare people.

Doesn't sound like a good way to make friends though does it?

After school I have to go back to class as, yet again, I've forgotten a letter to take home and I don't fancy a close meeting with a staple gun if Miss finds out. That's why I'm late leaving and why I notice Wally still at the gates and secretly signalling to me.

Us Red Socks have lots of secret signs which we can use for all sorts of things. This one tells me to be alert as an enemy is close.

There's lots of things the sign doesn't tell me, like which particular enemy it might be, or where to look but it's enough to make me become suddenly alert.

Nothing.

At least nothing out of the ordinary as far as I can see.

Wally pretends he'd just spotted me and wanders over.

"You've just missed him."

Obviously.

"Who?"

"I don't know."

That helps.

"I've not seen him before but he looked out of place and sort of suspicious. Tall chap, long dark hair and a beard."

That sounded a bit familiar but I can't remember where from.

The only man I know with a beard is Mr Brown who teaches in Year Six but even Wally would recognise him. The bald head sort of helps.

Even though I'm supposed to have this amazing memory according to Miss S, it sometimes hides things from me and I have to sneak up on it.

If I can't remember something then I have to try and stop searching for it in my mind and allow my brain to sort out the answer for itself. Sometimes the answer then pops up straight away but at other

times, like now, it might take a
bit longer.

I'll just have to wait.

Peter Marney

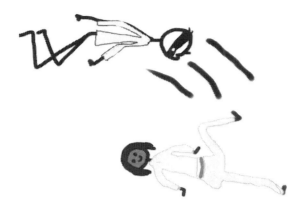

Age

I'm still going to judo after school and I think I must be getting a bit better because I'm hardly ending up on the floor at all.

Except for tonight.

Tonight I just can't keep my mind on anything.

I know that I generally try to stay fuzzy when I'm fighting so that I can sort of see everything at once and feel what my opponent is going to do next but tonight is different.

I guess I'm a bit annoyed at my brain because it won't tell me where I've seen Wally's mystery man before.

Sometimes you've got to look at things differently to get the answer.

It's like those pictures which you can see two different ways, like the one with the old witch and the young lady, or maybe like Keira's half empty glass. What you see depends on how you look at it.

I've just been thrown onto the floor again when I happen to look at Keira.

Now although I've known Keira for some time I don't really know much about her.

Yes, I know she's my babysitter and my judo teacher and my secret ninja leader and I know she's sort of crazy but I don't really know her like I know Red or Wally.

Does she have a baby sister or a big family?

I don't even know when her birthday is.

Then the thought strikes me, just after the floor hits me again.

I've always thought that Keira is a teenager because she looks so young but she can't be.

I mean, who's going to trust her with the keys to the school and let her run a judo class without any teachers present if she's just a teenager?

She must be older.

She must be a grown up like them or they wouldn't trust her would they?

It's about now that I get told off.

Keira has noticed how much I'm getting thrown about this evening.

"Jamie, stop messing about!"

What?

"If you let yourself be thrown one more time then you can get changed and go home and stop wasting my time."

That is so unfair.

How can I go home if she's got my key?

Does she expect me to break into my own bedroom?

Not that it would be a problem these days. The lock on my window is rubbish and wouldn't stop a two year old, assuming the baby was really good at climbing up to my window, which isn't that difficult.

Perhaps I need to stop thinking about Keira and start thinking about fighting so that I can stop being thrown about.

"Naz, swap partners and go practise with Jamie. Make him work."

That's all I need.

Now I'm going to be attacked by a Year Six girl.

Facing up to Naz as we grab each other's judo tops, she gives me a wink then starts jiggling for position so she can throw me.

It looks good but I don't think she's really trying. Instead she sort of half relaxes and lets me make an easy throw.

"Better Jamie."

The next time Naz makes it a bit more difficult but again ends up by letting me throw her.

"Come on Naz, he's not that good."

Thanks Keira.

Now Naz is really trying but so am I. This is going to be interesting.

Out of the corner of my eye I see that Keira is watching us carefully so I suppose I'd better not use some of the tricks that Red has taught me. After all, Naz is her friend and it wouldn't be fair.

Plus, Keira won't be happy either.

Judo is all about using the other person's strength to work against them. Get them to move their balance in one direction and then just give them a little nudge so they keep going until they hit the floor.

That's the idea anyway but neither of us are going to give in that easily and we both move from side to side trying to get the other person slightly off balance.

Then Naz sort of half stumbles and starts to fall backwards. As I'm holding onto her judo top I naturally follow her when, suddenly, she lifts her foot off of the floor, plants it on my chest and throws me over the top of her as she lands her back on the floor.

I'm so surprised that I roll back onto my feet without even thinking and turn to face Naz as she springs back up.

That was clever and now all I want is for Naz to teach me how to do it.

That's not going to happen tonight though as Keira has just told us to pack up and get changed.

"Jamie, as you've been slacking tonight you can help tidy up. Wally, you can help him."

Sounds like the Red Socks have some work to do tonight.

We end up without Red because she's having a sleep over at Naz's place. Those two are becoming real best friends.

Once Keira has checked that we have the school to ourselves, she explains that, so far, our cameras haven't caught anyone suspicious in school after hours so we need to do something different.

While we keep watch, she's going to make one of the enemy cameras stop working.

Keira explains that if one of our cameras stopped then we'd have to come and fix it, so she expects our mystery visitors to do the same.

All we now need to do is leave our cameras in position and watch.

On the way home I sneak glances at Keira, trying to work out how old she really is but I still haven't got a clue. I can mostly work out kids ages and what year they should be in but when it comes to grown ups I don't know where to start.

Well, that's not totally true.

Obviously old people are really old, and Mums and Dads are quite old and grandparents are ancient but that still leaves a lot of people stuck in the middle like Keira.

Maybe that's what they mean by middle aged although Miss says that the Middle Ages were a long time ago.

It's all very confusing.

I think I might have to find out some more about Kiera. I mean, I don't even know where she lives.

I think I may have to secretly follow her.

Peter Marney

Complaints

Some more people have written to our local newspaper complaining about our school and Keira reads the letters out to me.

She also reads something the editor has written which says that all these complains suggest that perhaps the right thing to do is close the school and move us all to other schools in the area.

This doesn't make sense.

What's the point in having a local school if it's not local?

At the moment we can all walk to school from the estate but, if they move it, we'd have to get a bus like they do for big school.

The Editor also says that there's lots of local support for closure.

It sounds like they've already made their minds up.

I don't think this is right and Keira says it all looks strange. Why has the local paper suddenly decided that we've got to close?

The inspectors report was bad but a lot of it wasn't really true and as for "lots of local support", nobody we know thinks it's a good idea.

In fact nobody can find anyone who doesn't like the school. So where is this so called support coming from?

I ask Miss after school and she agrees that it's a bit of a mystery so even the teachers can't understand what's going on.

Naz's Mums have started a petition, which is a letter signed by lots of people, saying that we're a good school and shouldn't be closed.

Lots of the local shops have copies of this letter so you can sign it when you go shopping and we ask Mr Patel if he can have a copy in his shop even though it's not really close to school.

"If your school can produce such polite children as you and your friends Jamie, then of course I'll help you."

I like Mr Patel.

The kids at the youth club are all talking about it as well.

A lot of the older ones used to go to our school and they think it's wrong to try and close us. Even Big Jay used to be at our school and he remembers Mr Brown when he had hair.

The trouble is that there doesn't seem to be much we can do about it. It's difficult to argue with people who don't seem to exist.

Either the people who want the school to close are too scared to speak up in public and only write anonymous letters or they want to stay hidden for some other reason.

Now why would that be?

This is beginning to remind me of our last adventure when some people were secretly trying to get the youth club thrown out of our home so that a rich man could build a new shopping centre and make a lot more money.

Even though we still had to move to this place when the coffee shop was sold, the rest of the block is still there as other local shopkeepers are making a big fuss.

Keira explains that they've gone to court which means that lawyers are now looking at everything carefully to explain why this new shop is supposed to be so good for the community.

Keira also tells me that our cameras haven't picked up anything unusual in school. Either our spies have forgotten abut their cameras or they're too busy to fix the fault.

The next day Miss S asks me to take a message to Mr Brown up in Year Six. She likes to get us to do this sort of thing so we can show how sensible we can be walking about the school.

While I'm standing by Mr Brown's desk waiting for him to write a reply to the message I happen to notice the grill on the wall.

Someone has moved it!

I know Keira moved it when she stopped the camera from working but she's clever enough to put the screws back exactly as they were before. Now, there's a bit more paint knocked off of one of the screws and the slots are all facing in different directions.

Yes, I know normal people don't remember this sort of thing but I do and someone else has taken that grill off.

"Wake up boy!"

Oops, I think Mr Brown is talking to me.

"Sorry Sir, I was just looking at the displays, they're really good."

That's not totally a lie but I think our's are better. It does get me out of trouble though.

"Well, when you're in Year Six you'll be able to do this sort of thing as well."

He's smiling so I think I said the right thing.

"Yes sir," I say as I take the message back to Miss S.

There's also a message I want to get to Kiera urgently if not sooner.

Peter Marney

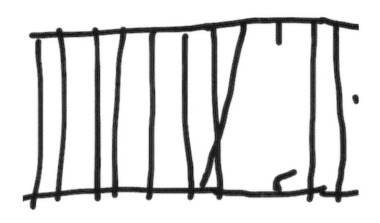

Sneaky

Someone's been stealing from our school again.

Last night Keira checked and every single enemy spy camera has gone.

How did they do that?

How did they manage to take all of their cameras out of those grills without our cameras seeing a thing?

That's clever but also a bit scary. These people are some serious ninjas.

Red manages to get rid of Naz in the playground so we're able to have a secret clan meeting.

Red goes first.

"What do we know? Not guess or think what happened. What do we really know?"

That's clever. Making us stop all our wild ideas and actually look at the evidence. That's exactly what Miss would make us do.

Wally counts on his fingers.

"No cars in the car park late at night, so they didn't use a car. Nothing showing from either entrance, so they can't have come through the doors and nothing showing in the main corridor."

This is a big problem but I've got an idea.

"What if it was one of our cameras going wrong? Would we just stroll in and replace it? Or would we think that an enemy might have tampered with it and so go in ninja style?"

Wally's got the same idea.

"So we break in through the windows of the classrooms, take our cameras and go out the same way. Through the hole in the fence and down the lane. Job done."

It's a great idea and exactly what I would do.

During the afternoon I convince myself that we've solved the mystery and I know just how to prove it.

If these spies make such a mess of the screws on the grills then maybe they might be a bit careless breaking in as well.

After school I pretend to remember I've forgotten my jumper. I think maybe I might have left it in the playground so it sort of makes sense to walk around the outside of the school to try and find it.

It's just a coincidence that I happen to walk past the windows of certain classes and why shouldn't I be looking carefully at the ground? After all, someone might have picked up my jumper and dropped it somewhere else.

Can't think of an excuse for looking carefully at the windows though.

I'm beginning to think this isn't such a good idea.

Nothing.

No scratch marks, no footprints, nothing.

Either our enemy ninjas are very, very good or I need to come up with a better idea.

I manage to catch up with Red on the way home and tell her the bad news. Obviously we're missing something.

"Why assume there's an enemy Jamie? We know about their cameras but they don't know about ours so why would they think that we exist?"

It's a good question.

"Wally said there's no cars in the car park at night but what about during the day. There's lots of cars around then."

She's got a point.

"And who's going to notice someone in the corridor who'd normally be there?"

Red's right but she's wrong as well.

"Red, what would happen if I came into the middle of one of your lessons and started to take the grill off of the wall?"

We both know that answer to that one so it must have been done when the classroom was empty or not being used.

That means at break or assembly times.

I think we need to look at our camera film with Keira again.

After school the next day I notice Naz's other mum in the playground going round with a copy of the petition and making sure that everyone has signed it.

Red says that they're now talking about organising a protest march to complain about the move to close the school.

I don't know how marching somewhere will solve the problem but I suppose it might show just how many people think it's a bad idea.

Names

I've looked at our camera films with Keira and it's really boring 'cos nothing much happens.

Even on fast forward it's still very, very boring.

There's lots going on but nothing out of the ordinary.

Maybe it's one of the teachers.

Maybe they're secretly filming themselves.

But that doesn't explain the cameras in the other classrooms and it'd stick out if one teacher was going into several different classrooms.

Mrs Wallace goes into lots of classrooms though.

We always see her popping into our room at least once a week just to say hello and to see what we're doing.

But that's stupid.

No way would Mrs Wallace want to spy on us when she can walk in and out when she wants.

It's still a mystery but I've got another idea which I share that night.

"Keira, what happens if that rich man with the shiny briefcase isn't allowed to build his new shop?"

Keira thinks that he'll have to go away and find some other town.

"But what if he really wants to build in this town? Could he find somewhere else to build? Somewhere a bit further out of town perhaps?"

You see, if it were me and I could make a lot of money from building a big shop then I'd still want to do it even if I had to find somewhere else.

I'd look for a nice big site nearby with lots of people with money to spend.

I know it's a daft idea but it would explain this sudden craze to close our school.

Not a secret committee deciding what comes after diabolos but a rich man wanting to get his way and make some more money from a nice big bit of land which happens to have a school built on it at the moment.

Keira thinks it's a daft idea.

Back in school I find I'm watching how people move around the school and who goes where.

Miss Northgate goes into all of the Year Five and Six classes but she's only here when we are and doesn't have time to play with any spy cameras.

All of our other visitors just come in to do whatever and then go again so that idea doesn't work either.

On the way to lunch I pass our caretaker helping the photocopier man bring in a new machine. After ages of it breaking down, someone has decided to replace the Year Six photocopier with a bigger model. I guess they do a lot of copying up in Year Six.

I wonder if I could fit inside a photocopier?

It's an easy way to secretly get into school and then I could sneak out at night and set up the spy cameras. Then they could come back

the next day and take the
photocopier and me away again.

Looking at it I don't think even
Red could fit into that small space.

Another idea gone.

After lunch we have to do a
special maths test and Miss helps
me by reading out the questions.

I'm really good at maths but
rubbish at reading so it sort of
makes sense for someone to read for
me so that I can show how good I am
at answering maths questions
without struggling to decode them
as well.

What I really need is something
like a small photocopier which you
can feed the paper in at one end
and instead of copying the page it
reads it out to you. That would be
cool.

At the end of the test Miss looks
pleased so I think I did well. The
last question was a bit tricky but
I'm sure I used the right method

even if I didn't get the right
answer.

Miss says that using the right
method and showing that you use it
is just as important as getting the
right answer so I hope she's right.

She usually is.

After school I go to play with Red
but she's off to see Naz so I tag
along.

This gives me a big problem.

What do I call Naz's mums?

I used to call Red's mum Mrs Pike
until I helped save Big Jay from
prison, then she said I was almost
part of the family and should call
her Aunty May. I still call Red's
dad Mr Pike but I don't see him
much.

The thing is though, what if both
Naz's mums are there? I can't call
them both "Mrs".

Ok, I have another problem as
well.

"Red, what's Naz's proper name?"

"Nazira, why?"

That helps a lot.

"No Red, I mean her surname."

"Jenkins. Why do you need to know her surname Jamie?"

I say I'm just curious and secretly decide to call both mums Mrs Jenkins. Hopefully only one of them will be there.

Their house is on the same road as mine but right at the other end of the estate so it's quite a walk.

Naz is pleased to see me and suggests we all play a computer game together.

I'm not really sure what girls play when they're on their own and grateful that I don't get made to join a dolls tea party or anything.

Mind you, I can't see either of these girls playing with dolls. Punch bags more likely.

I try calling Naz's mum Mrs Jenkins but she says to call her Joan which solves my problem I hope.

I'm in third place on the computer game so, when the other mum comes home, I'm ready to stop and say hello.

I shake hands and say "Mrs Jenkins" again but she tells me to call her Paula. This is all a lot easier than I was expecting and they're both really friendly.

Over tea we chat about our school and what's being done to fight the closure. I mention that Keira thinks some of the numbers in the report look a bit wrong and then I have to explain about Keira. Somehow I forget to mention the bit about her being a secret ninja leader or the amount of trouble she gets us into.

Paula is interested in these funny figures and asks if she can meet Keira so I have to write down

Paula's mobile number to pass on. Red makes sure I put the note in my pocket and the next day reminds me about it. Red knows what I'm like with notes.

Lucky for me, we haven't got time to finish our game so I don't really lose, just sort of half lose. I say thank you for tea and then jog home so that I'm in before Mum gets back from work.

I even remember to put the note somewhere safe for Keira's next visit.

Peter Marney

Juggling

Have I mentioned that Keira is really good with computers?

I found this out when she tried to help me with my homework a while back. When she found that we didn't have the internet at home she sort of borrowed the connection from next door without asking them.

Keira says they can check if anyone else is using their internet if they're bothered and anyway, using a password called "Pa55w0rd" is just asking for someone to hack it.

I'm only saying this because it shows that Keira can do things with computers that normal people can't. I've also found out that she's got friends who are even better at this sort of thing. They can find their way into your computer without you even knowing and then search for hidden stuff.

Keira doesn't explain the details but tells me that, because of her friends, we now know the name of at least someone who has been writing to the local paper as "an angry parent".

It might be a coincidence but this parent has exactly the same surname as our old deputy head, Mr Jenson. Not exactly a popular name and not exactly a popular teacher.

If it is him then I can think of one or two reasons why he would want to see our school closed.

Keira shows me the paper's website and some of the stuff they've been writing about our school. I recognise a photo of our playground and one of our corridor. I also notice the time on the school clock which tells me that it was taken not long after the end of our school day.

What is even more interesting is right at the edge of the picture. Most people wouldn't even notice or recognise it but then not many people would know what our cleaners trolleys look like.

When I stop bouncing up and down I manage to tell Keira my discovery.

All the time we've been looking for strange people coming into school and we forgot some of the people who actually work there all the time. Our caretaker can go wherever he wants in the school and

I guess the cleaners can do the same.

Keira flicks to another page on the newspaper website which shows the pictures of all of their reporters. I can't be certain but one of the women looks a bit familiar. Different hair colour and a lot prettier but she does look more than a bit like one of our cleaners. The one who, I now realise, I haven't seen for a couple of weeks.

I wonder if we've found our photographer?

It still doesn't explain why a newspaper would be spying on our school but at least we might be making some progress and the glass isn't still half empty.

Keira's very happy.

Apparently there are laws to stop people using secret cameras (now she tells me!) and especially cameras to take pictures of children. If they try to use any of this then the newspaper could be in serious trouble.

But why would the paper take such a risk? Surely the owners would stop their reporters doing anything so stupid. After all, they're not secret ninjas like us are they?

Then I ask a good question.

"Keira, does this website say who owns the paper?"

She goes to another page and then starts bouncing up and down just like me.

She says I've been really clever.

That doesn't sound like me at all.

It might be another coincidence but the paper's owner is a company with the same name as that rich man who wants to build his big shopping centre.

Maybe my daft idea isn't so stupid after all.

It's all very well knowing this stuff but the trouble is we're totally unable to prove anything and we're going to have to fight without knowing exactly who we're supposed to be fighting.

But at least we know we have an enemy.

If our rich man does own the newspaper then it makes sense that he'd want to show our school as failing so that he can step in and buy the land when we all have to move out.

That would explain those men who came to measure everything. If I was going to buy some land I'd want to make sure my new shopping centre could actually fit on it.

Then there's the mystery hairy man who Wally saw and who might be spying on me. Maybe he's working for the rich man as well.

But why would he spy on me?

Keira's beginning to wonder if our rich man might have paid our school inspectors to write that rubbish report about us.

Even if he didn't pay them all he could have just paid the one who wrote the final report.

Keira's also been talking to Paula about the numbers in the report. They both know about this statistics thing and how numbers can be juggled to produce different results.

I don't understand but Keira says it's just like the half empty glass. Juggle the numbers one way and they look bad; jiggle them the other way and they look ok.

Maybe all this juggling and jiggling numbers will make more sense when I'm in big school and someone starts teaching me this stuff.

Paula and Joan have been talking to lots of the mums and have organised a meeting at our school and invited the Education board who are the ones who decide whether to close us or not.

That's going to be an interesting meeting.

Surprise

Kids aren't really supposed to be at this meeting but Keira has sneaked me and Red in at the back. The hall is really crowded and nobody is going to notice us.

On the stage I can see Mrs Wallace and a couple of the people I've seen visiting the school before. I suppose these are the ones Keira was talking about.

The editor of the local newspaper is also sitting on stage next to our new deputy head. Near the front I can see lots of our teachers and there are loads of parents from the estate, including most of the Pikes who could probably make up an audience just on their own.

Mrs Wallace stands up and welcomes everyone to the meeting. She explains that we're here to understand why there's a call to close our school. She then asks one of the important men in a suit to go through the inspectors report and say what the problems are.

This is really boring but when he's finished, Mrs Wallace asks if there are any questions and it gets interesting again.

Miss S stands up and asks about the school's Maths results.

"There's several children in my class who have problems reading."

I know at least one of them.

It's me.

"And I see that all their results are in with the rest which doesn't seem fair."

Some others agree.

"As these figures are based on last year's results I gave my current class the same test but read the questions out to those with reading problems. Then I marked the test, and the class results were ten percent above the national average. So, if we're testing maths ability and not reading ability then we seem to be doing rather well."

The man in the suit disagrees.

"Those figures are irrelevant. You say yourself that you helped the children."

He's interrupted by Mr Patel who I didn't realise was here.

Unfortunately I can't understand a single word of Mr Patel's question and by the look on his face neither can the suit man.

Then something changes and I can understand again.

"I'm sorry you didn't understand my comment sir but, you see, I was speaking in Hindi, my own language. I suppose you not understanding it is like someone who can't read trying to do a Maths paper when nobody is translating for them. As I understand it, this teacher was merely translating and not helping the pupils to answer the questions. So I think the results are very relevant."

Everybody starts clapping for some reason and Mr Patel sits down.

Naz's mum Paula then starts attacking the numbers as well and somehow proves that a lot of the report is rubbish if you compare it to the school's own figures.

Mr Suit argues that our school information is confidential but Paula tells him that she works for some special office and is allowed to see these figures to check that people don't try and tell lies with numbers.

That sort of shuts him up.

About now the editor of our local paper tries to support the closing of our school.

Bad move.

Aunty May stands up with a big bundle of papers.

"This is a statement signed by every parent in the school, every one of them, saying that they've not said any of the things printed in your newspaper or used in the report. So either someone is making things up or you aren't checking that these letters come from real parents. Which is it?"

That's the sort of question where you can't answer either way without getting into trouble. You can tell she's a mum.

Mrs Wallace gets the editor out of trouble and starts talking about our reading results. Again the test scores for those of us who can't read well are mixed in with everything else and the school is actually doing a lot better than the report says.

"So, we have a report which uses incorrect figures, a parent survey which is totally made up, and several newspaper reports which have been written without checking the facts."

That seems a good way of putting it.

"I think everyone will agree that this so called evidence is very weak indeed and, unless there's a secret motive somewhere for closing the school, we've proved our case to stay open. A proper inspection using the correct figures would show this to be an excellent school."

This is where everyone stands up and claps and I can't see what's happening. It doesn't matter though because that's the end of the meeting.

I thought the editor didn't say too much but I didn't know until later that he'd had an email suggesting a link between his company and a certain well known rich man.

This email also reminded him of the laws concerning spying on children and asked for a comment on why one of his reporters had been working as a cleaner at our school.

The email was signed from "An angry parent" but I don't think it came from Mr Jenson. More likely it was from Keira or one of her clever computer friends.

I expect the newspaper will now quietly drop their campaign against our school and find a new craze to write about.

The next day Mrs Wallace announces in assembly that our school report is being ignored as it has got too many mistakes in it.

We're staying open.

The diabolo craze has also ended and it's safe again to walk on the school field.

I'm down by the far edge when I spot the hairy man standing outside the school fence and looking towards the climbing frame.

Why is he still here? Hasn't he heard that our school isn't for sale?

Carefully I edge towards the bushes and use their cover to sneak closer.

He still hasn't spotted me and I'm able to creep really close and get a good look at him if he turns around.

Suddenly he notices me.

"Hello Jamie."

I'm shocked.

Now I know why he looked so familiar.

It's Dad!

The End

Peter Marney

The next book in the series

Why has Jamie got a new uncle and why does everyone end up hiding in bushes?

Suddenly, things get very serious and the Clan are threatened by an enemy who can destroy them forever.

Have they met a force they cannot defeat and will it ruin their future together?

Peter Marney

About the author

Peter Marney lives by the sea, is just as bad at drawing as Jamie, and falls over if his socks don't have the right day of the week written on them.

On a more serious note, Peter has worked supporting children with reading difficulties and understands some of their problems. He is passionate about the importance of both reading and storytelling to the growing mind.

Peter Marney

The Red Sock Ninja Clan Adventures

Birth of a Ninja

Jamie's about to start another new school and has been told to stay out of trouble. Like that's going to happen!

It's not as if he wants to fight but you've got to help out if a girl's being picked on, right? Even if it does turn out that she's the best fighter in the school and laughs at your odd socks.

Follow Jamie as he makes friends, sorts out a big problem at his school, and discovers that his weird new babysitter knows secret ninja skills.

Hide and Seek

Find out why Jamie hates dogs and why he's hiding in a school cupboard in the dark. Has it got something to do with Keira's new training games for the Red Sock Ninjas?

The Mystery Intruder

Someone is playing in school after dark and it's not just the Red Sock Ninjas. Maybe Harry knows who it is but he's not talking so Jamie will have to find another way to solve this mystery.

The Mighty Porcupine

What do you do when your enemy is too powerful to fight? Has somebody finally beaten the Red Sock Ninjas?

The Mystery Troublemakers

Someone wants to get Jamie's new youth club into trouble but why?

Maybe the Red Sock Ninjas can find the answer by climbing rooftops or will it just get them into more trouble?

Statty Sticks

Why is Jamie being attacked by a small girl who isn't Red and why does he get the feeling that someone is spying on him?

Has it got anything to do with why his school is in danger and how numbers can lie?

Enemies and Friends

Why has Jamie got a new uncle and why does everyone end up hiding in bushes?

Have the Red Sock Ninjas now found too big a porcupine and will it spell disaster for their future together?

Run Away Success

Where do you run to when everything goes wrong? That's the latest problem for the Red Sock Ninjas and this time Wally isn't around to mastermind the plan.

With the enemy closing in for capture, the friends must split up and disappear. Is this the end of the Clan or the beginning of a whole new experience for Jamie?

Rise and Shine

Why does going to the library get Jamie into a fight and what's that got to do with Keira's plan for getting rid of him?

Helping to put on a show with Miss G was difficult enough without guess who turning up. Yet again the Red Socks must use their skills to save the day and the show.

Rabbits and Spiders

Has Red set up Jamie on a date with Dog Girl? If so, why is he now running around in circles? Maybe it's got something to do with the fact that the enemy have at last found them again.

The Red Sock Ninjas must use all of their skills in this last adventure if they are to escape and live happily ever after.

Printed in Great Britain
by Amazon